1990 To Olivia: Merry Christmas with Love — Jan, Carrie & TJ.

THE CHRISTMAS LAMB

THE CHRISTMAS LAMB

ANNE BAIRD

Morrow Junior Books / New York

Library of Congress Cataloging-in-Publication Data
Baird, Anne.
The Christmas lamb.
Summary: A young sheep who feels neglected at
Christmas tries several attention-getting tactics,
such as disguising himself as a reindeer, with
unfortunate results.
[1. Sheep—Fiction.   2. Christmas—Fiction]
I. Title.
PZ7.B1618Ch 1989   [E]   88-5137
ISBN 0-688-07774-9
ISBN 0-688-07775-7 (lib. bdg.)

FOR RUTH AND CHRIS BREUKELMAN,
MY WONDERFUL MUM AND DAD

It was Christmas Eve, and no one had visited the zoo all day.

"Why don't the children like us anymore?" asked Scuffy. "Why do they like reindeer and Santa better?"

"They don't," said his father, "except at Christmas."

"They'll come back when the fun is over," said his mother. "Now go to sleep like a sweet sheep."

But Scuffy didn't *want* to sleep. He didn't *want* to miss the Christmas fun.

He waited till his parents fell asleep, then climbed the fence.

"If the children don't want *sheep* at Christmas," he decided, "I'll be a reindeer."

He tied two branches to his head, then rushed off to join the reindeer in Grundy's windows.

The revolving door of Grundy's store was spinning like a top.
Scuffy sprang in, but...

SKREEEEKKK!
His "horns" got stuck and jammed the door.
The store manager had to call the Fire Department!

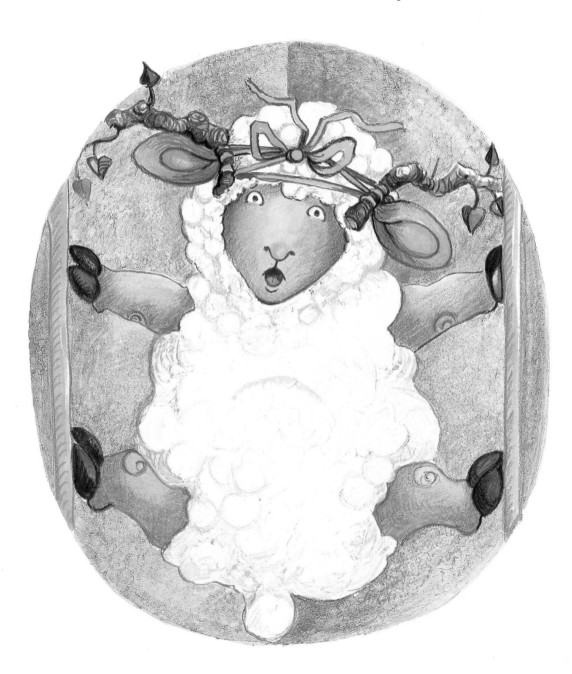

The fire fighters pried the doors open. The people rushed out.
But Scuffy was frightened by the noise and ran away.

Around the corner, where he hid, he spied a Christmas poster. It showed Santa bringing toys to happy children.

"*That's* why people like Santa better than sheep and reindeer," cried Scuffy. "He brings them *treats!*"

Children brought Scuffy treats at the zoo and he loved them.

A Santa Claus dummy was standing by the door of Slotnicks store.
He was dressed in a bright red suit and shiny boots.

This gave Scuffy an idea.

"I'll be a Santa sheep! *Everyone* will love me then."

Scuffy pulled the clothes off the dummy and put them on. "I'll bring them back," he promised.

"Now for the treats!"

Scuffy had no money to buy treats. But he found lots of goodies that people had thrown away.

So he loaded a clean, green garbage bag...

and trotted off down the street.

"A short house with a fat chimney is what I need," he puffed,
"and there it is."

Up the fire escape he crept.
His boot slipped and his bag tripped
him, but still he climbed.

HELP!

The chimney was too thin and Scuffy was too fat.

"*Schleerrrpp!*" he gurgled.

He sucked in his tummy as hard as he could. He squeezed himself into the chimney and fell . . .

into the Foster family's fireplace. His Santa suit caught on a
nail, and he hung, kicking and jerking, like a puppet on a string.

"What's *that*?" cried the children, staring at the dancing boots.

"I don't know," said Mr. Foster. "We'd better find out."

Mr. Foster heaved on Scuffy's legs, trying to pull him loose.

FLOOM!

Scuffy popped free. Black soot exploded into the room with him. His bag burst, and the Christmas treats shot around the room like soccer balls.

"YEEIIPE!" yelled the Fosters.
"*BAAAAAA!*" cried Scuffy as he fled.

"Everything I do goes wrong," he said, weeping. "I can't even keep my promise to return Santa's clothes." Scuffy had never felt so sad.

"Christmas is no time for sheep. I'd better give up and go home to bed, like Mama said."

Scuffy started toward the zoo. But he was tired from trying to have Christmas fun. He passed a little church. Light streamed through the stained glass windows. Music crept from beneath the wooden doors. The church garden was very peaceful.

"I'll just rest a moment," murmured Scuffy.
He flopped in a pile of fresh-smelling hay and shut his eyes.
In a minute, he was fast asleep.

Not for long, though. He woke surrounded by children singing Christmas carols. Many of them were his friends from the zoo!

Scuffy was happy to be part of the fun at last. He jumped up and knocked over *another* lamb. But this lamb didn't move. He was made of wood!

"Look," cried Jenny, "one of the lambs in the creche has come *alive*!"

"No, it's *Scuffy*," said Amanda. "But he should be home in bed at the zoo."

"*Baaa*," agreed Scuffy. He was having fun at last. But it was long past his bedtime.

The children tied a ribbon around Scuffy's neck. They walked him back to the zoo, singing carols all the way.

When anyone asked them, "What's going on?" they said, "We're taking our Christmas lamb home to bed."

"Good-bye, Scuffy," they called as they left the zoo. "See you soon."

"What's going on?" mumbled Scuffy's father sleepily.

"It's a long story," replied Scuffy with a yawn. "May I tell you tomorrow?"

"Tomorrow will do," said his mother. "Now go to sleep like a sweet sheep."

And this time, Scuffy did.